ARNOLD LOBEL

Odd Owls & Stout Pigs

A Book of Nonsense

COLOR BY **ADRIANNE LOBEL**

HARPER

An Imprint of HarperCollinsPublishers

Odd Owls & Stout Pigs: A Book of Nonsense

Copyright © 2009 by the Estate of Arnold Lobel

Printed in the U.S.A.

For information address HarperCollins Children's Books, a division of HarperCollins Publishers,

10 East 53rd Street, New York, NY 10022.

www.harpercollinschildrens.com

Library of Congress Cataloging-in-Publication Data

Lobel, Arnold.

    Odd owls & stout pigs : a book of nonsense / Arnold Lobel ; color by Adrianne Lobel. — 1st ed.

        p.   cm.

    Summary: Presents a linked collection of brief rhymes featuring owls and pigs.

    ISBN 978-0-06-180054-2 (trade bdg.) — ISBN 978-0-06-180055-9 (lib. bdg.)

    [1. Stories in rhyme.   2. Owls—Fiction.   3. Pigs—Fiction.]   I. Lobel, Adrianne, ill.   II. Title.

PZ8.3.L82Od   2009   2009001406

[E]—dc22   CIP

                                                                            AC

Typography by Martha Rago

09 10 11 12 13 LPR 10 9 8 7 6 5 4 3 2 1 ❖ First Edition

For Crosby and George
—Arnold Lobel

For Ruby and her grandfather
—Adrianne Lobel

This owl blows up a big balloon.
He blows it till it breaks.
He doesn't mind at all because
He likes the pop it makes.

This owl is on a holiday.
He's jumping into lakes.
He's always very wet because
He likes the splash it makes.

While sitting at supper,
This owl makes a mess.
"I have ruined my appearance!"
He cries with distress.
"In spreading the butter
On top of my bread,
It seems I have buttered
My necktie instead."